A ·—

B —···

C —·—·

D —··

E ·

F ··—·

G ——·

H ····

I ··

J ·———

K —·—

L ·—··

M ——

N —·

O ———

P ·——·

Q ——·—

R ·—·

S ···

T —

U ··—

V ···—

W ·——

X —··—

ANNA DESNITSKAYA is the illustrator of *The Apartment: A Century of Russian History* (Abrams), *Gina from Siberia* (Animal Media Group), and many other books for young readers. In 2018, she was nominated for the Astrid Lindgren Memorial Award, a global award honoring creators' contributions to children's literature. A native of Moscow, Russia, Anna now lives in northern Israel with her family. Follow her on Instagram @anyadesnitskaya.

LENA TRAER is a freelance Russian- and English-language translator with a focus on books for children and young adults. Her past projects include translating *Wind: Discovering Air in Motion* (Eerdmans) and *How to be your dog's best friend* (Thames & Hudson) into English and translating a variety of scientific materials and picture books into Russian. Born and raised in Siberia, Russia, Lena now lives in San Francisco.

Anna Desnitskaya

ON THE EDGE
OF THE WORLD

Translated by Lena Traer

To my sister, Dasha.
— A. D.

EERDMANS BOOKS FOR YOUNG READERS

GRAND RAPIDS, MICHIGAN

Kamchatka Peninsula

Kamchatka crab
1 m (3.3 ft) long

Brown bear

BERING SEA

SEA OF
OKHOTSK

KLYUCHEVSKAYA SOPKA
The highest active volcan
of Eurasia

There are
no snakes
on Kamchatka at all!

PACIFIC OCEAN

Reindeer

PETROPAVLOVSK-KAMCHATSKY
The capital of Kamchatka
Population: 180,000

Tufted
puffin

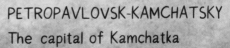

Seal

Walrus

AVERAGE TEMPERATURE
July: +12°C (53.6°F)
January: -8°C (17.6°F)

Hi, I'm Vera. I live on the eastern coast of the Kamchatka Peninsula in Russia. There's only the Pacific Ocean to the east of us. My mom says that we're on the real edge of the world.

When I was little, I asked her, "Mom, what does that mean— the edge of the world? What's out there, beyond the edge?" She laughed and said that "the edge of the world" was just an expression, because the Earth is actually round like a ball. And if you left from our edge of the world—Kamchatka—and sailed across the Pacific Ocean for a long, long time, you'd eventually reach another country, somewhere like Chile.

My Most Valuable Things

FEATHER COLLECTION

чайка

бекас

FLASHLIGHT

A SMALL BIRD SKULL
THAT I FOUND ON THE BEACH

Лев, колдунья
и платяной шкаф

MY FAVORITE BOOK:
*THE LION, THE WITCH
AND THE WARDROBE*

MY FAVORITE FOOD:
GRANDMA'S *SYRNIKI*
(COTTAGE CHEESE
PANCAKES)!

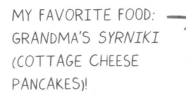

THIS IS MY MOM

She is very smart and so funny. When I was little, she studied early childhood education in college, and now she is a preschool teacher.

When I grow up, I want to be a ship captain.

 CAPTAIN'S CAP

Last year, I learned how to tie knots. I also learned Morse code— this is a method of communication that uses a series of dots and dashes to relay information. When I become a captain, I will sail from our edge of the world to Chile!

CAPSTAN KNOT

SQUARE KNOT

FLEMISH BEND

More than anything in this world, I wish I had a
real friend. For some reason, I don't have one yet.

My mom says:

Just go up to someone at school or at the playground and say, "Let's be friends!"

I don't answer, but I think that this is ridiculous. I'm not four years old.

Grandma says:

Don't worry, you're going to find a friend sooner or later.

I shrug. Sooner or later . . . and when would that be exactly?

It's a school break, which means no alarm clock today. Instead, I wake up to the sounds drifting in from the kitchen: a softly mumbling TV, clinking dishes, and sizzling butter—Grandma is frying *syrniki.*

Our kitchen feels quite cramped, but there is enough room at the table for the three of us—Mom, Grandma, and me. We could even fit in one more person.

Mom eats while reading the news on her phone, and Grandma watches the weather forecast on the TV, piling more *syrniki* on our plates.

After breakfast, I go outside to walk my dog, Mukha (her name means "fly").

I throw her the ball, and she brings it back. If I'm too slow and don't throw the ball right away, she gets impatient and starts to bark.

I throw a tennis ball as far as I can, and Mukha brings it back to me over and over again.

After lunch, I play on a tablet in Grandma's room.

A while back, when I saw *The Hobbit,*
I got the idea of going on a long journey
in my favorite video game, just like Bilbo
and the dwarves. I've already prepared
the necessary supplies:

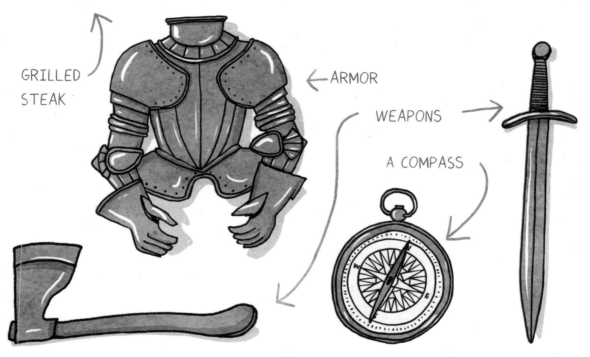

GRILLED
STEAK

←ARMOR

WEAPONS →

A COMPASS

It would be useful to have a horse for this journey,
but I don't know how to tame one.

Recently, my mom taught me how to make a *sekretik*,
a little secret treasure. Here's how you do it:

1 Dig a little hole
in the ground.

2 Line it with tinfoil.

3 Put all the pretty
things you have
into the hole: beads,
flowers, buttons.

4 Cover it with
a nice piece of
colored glass. It will
be like a magic window.

It's called "secret" because you can't tell anyone about it,
only your closest friends.

If I had a friend, I'd definitely show them my *sekretik* under the alder tree, with its blue glass, a LEGO minifigure, and forget-me-nots.

In the evening, I go to the beach with my mom and
Mukha. I stand beside the ocean and dream: *What if
I had a friend over there, beyond the edge of the world?*
I take a flashlight out of my pocket and shine it over
the dark water. I turn it on and off and on again:
Dot dot dot dot. Dot dot. This is Morse code for "hi."
I keep flashing the light on the dark shore: *Hi, I'm Vera.*
Hi, I'm Vera.

My mom says that the flashlight is too weak to send signals across the ocean. But I know she is wrong, because today I saw a response: *Hi, I'm Lucas.*

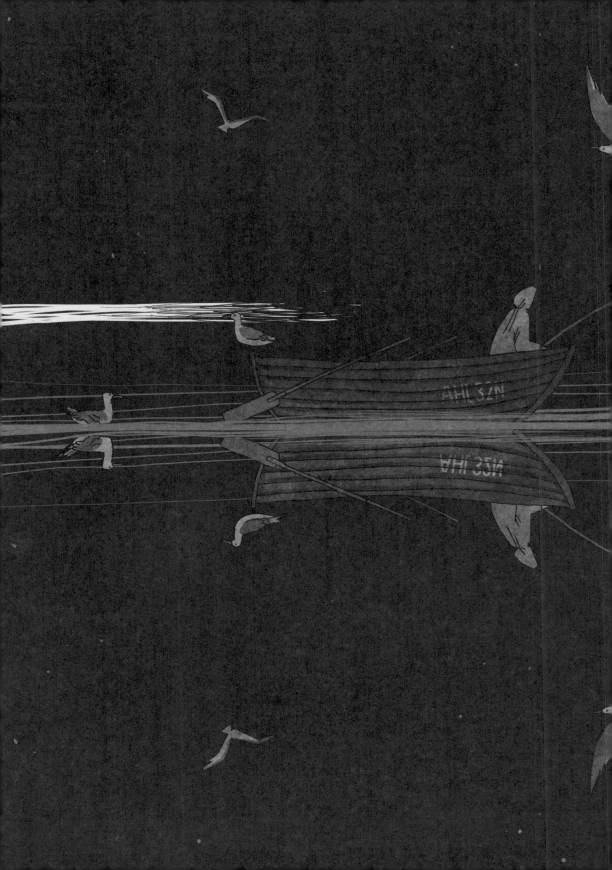

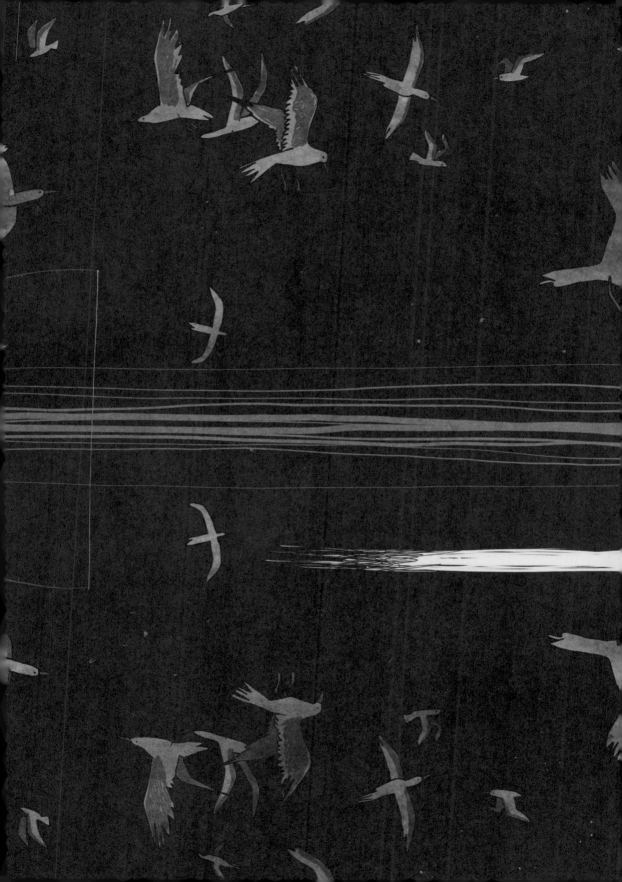

I know that according to all
the laws of physics, light from my
flashlight can't reach the other end of the
world, but still I send signals every night.
And today I finally saw a response: Hi, I'm Vera.

In the evening, Dad
and I go to the beach.
With my flashlight, we can
see fishing boats pulled up on
the sand. I imagine: What if I had
a friend over there, beyond the edge
of the world? I point my flashlight into the
darkness and blink in Morse code: four short flashes,
pause, and then two short flashes again: Dot dot dot
dot. Dot dot. This is how you say "hi." I keep flashing the
light on the dark shore: Hi, I'm Lucas. Hi, I'm Lucas.

I build a big house in the game. Then I come across wild horses in a nearby forest and randomly discover that I can tame them if I feed them hay.

If I had a friend, I'd definitely tell them about this. And I would also show them our old tree and the most comfortable branch.

Before dinner, Dad lets me play my
favorite video game on his laptop.

I'm so comfortable here, like I'm sitting in an armchair, and there's even room for one more person on the branch next to me. I open the book to the first page and start reading:
"Once there were four children whose names were Peter, Susan, Edmund and Lucy."

After lunch, I help my mom put the dirty dishes in the dishwasher, grab a new book—a gift from my grandmother—and go outside.

There is an old tree in our garden. I kick off my shoes, take the book in one hand, and

grab a low-hanging branch with the other. Then I get a grip on the bark with my toes,

pull myself up, and settle in a fork of the tree.

There's no one here, so I practice by myself. I stand in one goal area and try to score a goal in the opposite net. Cold wind blows from the ocean, and soccer isn't meant to be played alone.

Still, I stay on the field for a long time, kicking the ball into the goal over and over again.

After breakfast, my mom and sisters go outside for a walk, and I grab a ball and go to a soccer field near my new school.

I pour myself a cup of hot chocolate and drink it alone in the doorway, wrapping myself up in Dad's shirt.

Today I wake up early, even though it's the weekend.

I go to the kitchen. Everyone is still asleep except for Dad, who is already sitting at the kitchen table and working on his laptop. He looks up with an absent-minded smile and says:

Good morning, *niño!*

before looking at the screen again.

I hear a scratching sound. It's our cat, Nero, asking to be let in. I go to the back door, open it, and our shivering cat slips inside the house. For the first time in a while, it's a beautiful sunny morning, but I can still feel the winter-like cold and dampness.

Grandma asks on a video call:

Have you made
any friends, *mi amor?*

"Not yet, Grandma,"
I answer.

My dad says:

When you start at your new school,
you'll make new friends!

To be honest, I'm not so sure about that. At my old school
in Santiago, I didn't really have any friends either.

THIS IS MY DAD

He is a marine biologist. He spends his days
writing his thesis. Several times a year he sails
on an ocean expedition ship. I can't go with
him, but he taught me Morse code, like
what sailors use—each letter in this special
alphabet is formed by an arrangement
of dots and dashes.

MY FAVORITE BOOK:
THE HOBBIT

J.R.R. Tolkien
EL HOBBIT

I want to be a paleontologist. Just recently,
fossils of a new dinosaur species have been
found in Chile! Paleontologists called it *ARACKAR
LICANANTAY* and it is six meters (twenty feet) long!

My Most Valuable Things

AMMONITE FOSSILS
that I found on the beach.
They are millions and
millions of years old!

SOCCER BALL

FLASHLIGHT

MY FAVORITE FOOD:
HAMBURGER!

When we lived in Santiago, I ate hamburgers every week, but I doubt there are any burger joints here, on the edge of the world. My mom says she can make me a burger at home, but you know it's just not the same.

Hi, I'm Lucas, and I live in Chile. We used to live in Santiago, the capital. When my father changed jobs, we moved to a small town on the coast.

On Saturdays we call my grandmother, and every time she seems upset, grumbling, "Look where you are! It's the real edge of the world!" When Grandma first said this, my younger sisters got scared: "What do you mean—the edge of the world? Is there really nothing there, beyond the ocean? Does it just flow off the edge of the Earth into space?" I laughed at them, "No, silly, everyone knows that's just an expression. The Earth is round like a ball and has no edges. If you sailed from our home across the Pacific Ocean for a long, long time, you'd eventually reach Australia or China or Russia. That's all."

Chile

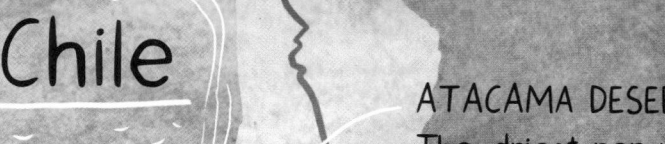

ATACAMA DESERT
The driest non-polar desert in the world

Chile is the world's most stretched-out country. It measures 4,630 km (2,880 mi) from north to south and only 430 km (265 mi) from west to east!

← Andean condor

SANTIAGO
The capital of Chile
Population: 6,000,000

Llama

Humpback whale

Flamingo

PACIFIC OCEAN

Armadillo

Dolphin

AVERAGE TEMPERATURE

North
January: +24°C (75.2°F)
July: +16°C (60.8°F)

ATLANTIC OCEAN

South
January: +18°C (64.4°F)
July: +9°C (48.2°F)

Magellanic penguins

Anna Desnitskaya

ON THE EDGE
OF THE WORLD

Translated by Lena Traer

To my husband, Grisha.
— A. D.

Text and illustrations © 2023 Anna Desnitskaya

Published by arrangement with Debbie Bibo Agency
Original book design by Alice Nussbaum

English-language translation © 2023 Lena Traer

First published in the United States in 2023 by Eerdmans Books for Young Readers,
an imprint of Wm. B. Eerdmans Publishing Co., Grand Rapids, Michigan

www.eerdmans.com/youngreaders

32 31 30 29 28 27 26 25 24 23   1 2 3 4 5 6 7 8 9 10

ISBN 978-0-8028-5612-8 ✳ A catalog record of this book is available from the Library of Congress.

Illustrations created digitally.

The book and product names referenced are the property of their respective owners.